The Dwelling-Place

'A man's religion is the form of mental rest, or dwelling-place, which, partly, his fathers have gained or built for him, and partly, by due reverence to former custom, he has built for himself; consisting of whatever imperfect knowledge may have been granted, up to that time, in the land of his birth, of the Divine character, presence, and dealings; modified by the circumstances of surrounding life.'

JOHN RUSKIN, *Val d'Arno*

Clive Wilmer

The Dwelling-Place

Carcanet · Manchester

ACKNOWLEDGEMENTS

Some of these poems appeared in *Shade Mariners* (Cambridge, 1969), Faber *Poetry Introduction II*, *Ten English Poets* (Carcanet, 1976); and in the magazines *Southern Review, PN Review, Converse, Pawn, Poetry Nation, Spectator* and *Caret*, to whose editors thanks are due.

SBN 85635 232 2

First published in 1977 by
Carcanet New Press Limited
330 Corn Exchange
Manchester M4 3BG

Second Printing 1981

The publisher acknowledges the financial assistance of
the Arts Council of Great Britain.

Printed and Bound by Short Run Press Ltd.,
Exeter, Devon.

CONTENTS

To the memory of my father and my maternal grandparents

—*Aspiciens a longe*—

THE DEDICATION

E. W., 1882-1948

It was your room they moved me to
    (I, not yet four the year you died,
    Not grasping how I might have cried),
Dear Father, whom I hardly knew;

And your great, polished chest-of-drawers
    Was all that I inherited
    Besides: it loomed above my bed:
Dark in the wood-grain still there pours,

In memory, vast, the gathered deep—
    Huge waves that surged, curded to foam
    (In the security of home),
And broke, as I sank into sleep.

Clearing those drawers out, grown to man,
    I came upon your photograph:
    It seemed a visual epitaph
To one I never thought, till then,

I'd loved or feared. Now time had blurred
    Your placid features, void of care,
    Who died, as if you had no heir,
Intestate: so on me conferred

No such authority as dressed,
    In my conception, all your acts;
    Mere rooms to occupy as facts—
No freehold rightfully possessed.

Moreover, childish hands, untaught
    In every art but innocence,
    Had scribbled into radiance
The aspect which the lens had caught

And overlaid its sepia hue—
    Your clothes now black and gold; your face
    Crimson; the sky (your dwelling-place),
Empty, was touched with purest blue—

As if a fatherless naïf,
    Dreaming a different element,
    Within the oval frame had meant
To translate his confused belief

Into pictorial commentary:
    This was the palimpsest I'd scrawled
    Glimpsing a King, beyond my world,
Who governed from across the sea.

Your power you held but to resign—
    A rationally gentle reign;
    I see you smiling, mild again,
Whose failing life engendered mine;

And through my childhood dreams, that face
    Taught what a child could never see:
    That I must never hope to be
The master of my dwelling-place.

                            1975

I
PROLOGUE
(1965-1970)

THE EXILE

I threw up watchtowers taller than my need
With bare walls the enemy could not scale,
I wrenched stone from the near country-side
And built my city on the highest hill;
    Over the land I scarred I reared
Impenetrable the walls and citadel.

Then to approach the city from afar
All you could see was soaring, there was such peace
Knowing the city mine I lay secure.
My own, one night, woke me—every face
    A jutting rock relief in glare,
The torchlight that illumined new distress.

They lit me into darkness. The harsh sun
—My understanding dazzled when it dawned—
Disclosed me vulnerable. I stumbled on,
Till blown, a sterile seed, by years like wind
    Indifferent guidance, I am set down
Among familiar stone in a changed land.

Now it is only details I perceive:
The towers lopped, stone interspersed with weed
In patches; a deeper speckling seems to give
Form to the complex of decay, but is fled
    With a lizard flicker. Poppies revive,
In the wall they spatter, spectres of old blood.

CHIAROSCURO

Chiaroscuro: abandoned dark
Falling back before the advancing light.
If the room I live in were not so vast
The light I hold would cancel the black
Out there, that dissipates my range of sight.

To banish darkness, first you must plumb
The darkness' depth—and nothing known more deep.
I know true darkness is much more
Than interrupted light—shadow clung
To the thing's edge—or the domain of sleep.

I have known times when the mind cracks before
The force of its own thoughts. With those
Moments in mind he has taken a lamp
To cast a light on the future's flickering floor;
Behind his back, the gates of darkness close.

Behind his back, the gates of darkness close;
The leap he takes is into light's abyss,
Knowing that at the brink one never knows
Whether it's darkness that encloses
Light, or the light darkness.

He takes a chance on what may lie in store
For him in landscapes where the objects glow:
In my world where the darkness breeds around me,
Light may open up a world beyond me.
Opening outward, opening more and more.

THE INVALID STORYTELLER

I.

The house he lived in was always (a little) dark,
A kind old man who told us, children, stories
—Or old he seemed to us, and like his stories
    Like his house, and kind; we'd shirk

Church on a Sunday, run to his house, and leap
Two at a time up the eight stone steps to reach
For the brass door-knocker, knock, then turn the latch,
    And penetrate the gloom; we'd creep

Soft up the deepening stream of red that flushed
Obscure in the carpeted stairs, and only shadows
—From the almost-light of the front-door's frosted windows—
    Rose in the first-floor mirror; we'd push

Open an outer door and feel our way
Through curtained dark (we could smell the musty walls)
To tap at the inner room. A voice would call
Faint from the exile where his weakness lay.

II.

Lace, we remember, faded lace
To filter light and veil the panes
    Against the external day.
The light was inter-meshed with lace
Upon the wall, fastidious,
In patterns subtle as decay
    And intricate as pain:
Like pinks and greens on carcasses,
Like wrinkles on an old man's face.

Beyond our reach, above the veil
Where knowledge knit with pain and death
   Shimmered, the sun's rays
Burst through the panes and cast a pale
Rectangular frieze upon the wall,
Whose colours told of summer days,
   Whose pallor told of death;
Where he could watch what he recalled
Advancing, as he told each tale.

III.

   He lay immersed in shadows; there,
   One by one with a firm embrace
—Though little more than a voice that murmured stories—
   The old man welcomed us.
We remember still the clear blue-eyed stare
Which saw behind (we believed) the greeted face.

   He spoke; and when he told us how
   He fell in love with the fair princess
He had rescued, from a dragon, with his sword,
   We believed his every word.
But love (he said) had been unfulfilled, and now
Of sword and armour he lay dispossessed.

   Each tale of hero and princess
   He told would reach its happy end
At first; but as the weeks of summer browned
   He loosed his weary mind
On Hamlet's solitude and Ophelia's loss,
Parsifal's waste land, Philoctetes' wound.

   Much, we forget. (For innocence,
   Belief is not so hard.) Instead,
Fixed in the mind, now, is the man's plight—
   His gaze fixed on the light,
Longing toward it with his every sense.
We remember this much more than what he said.

The winter fell. And now we heard
　Most often as the sun turned bronze
Of how on Balder's heart a shadow fell;
　　He stared hard at the wall
As though at a waste of ice where warriors rode
With fire and sword in the blood of setting suns.

IV.

Perhaps we began to fear him
A little, we cannot say.

We climbed the stairs one Sunday,
Tapped on the sick-room door and whispered 'Sir?'
But waiting for no answer

Entered, to find him upright, his mouth hung open
As if to speak, and his eyes, not in welcome,
Fixed in a fearful stare on the wide wall

Where he saw his warriors come
And the shadow fall.

THE SPARKING OF THE FORGE

Stiffened and shrunk by age my grandfather
Leans forward now, confined within his chair,
Straining to raise a finger to point back
Over his shoulder, scarcely able to look
Over his shoulder through the darkening window
At the road behind him and before me where

The mailcoach ran just seventy years ago—
He suddenly tells me, reaching to capture one
Glimpse of the road where memory finds its form
And in whose lamps so many memories burn:
The armed guard in the rear, behind bars—
Changing the horses at the road's end inn—

And where we buy his tobacco every day
Was once the blacksmith's forge. I watch him stare
Into the crumbling coal and feel the blaze
Flare in the ancient forge and his childhood-eyes;
And whether the shoes were hammered on red-hot
Uncertain now, he recollects their glare.

His words uncertain now I watch him see
Bright in his mind the sparking of the forge,
The monstrous anvil and the sizzling steel,
The raising of the hammer high to feel
What once he had of muscle in his arm,
The hammer's beat sounding his deepest urge.

Each time recalled another fragment lost,
Still his past seeps back—with broken breath—
Continuous in a stream of memories.
I pick up only broken images:
Confined by time, as he is by his age,
My own time's loss I find in his lost youth.

An old man's death becomes a young man's rage;
I seize the coal-tongs; now the blacksmith's clamp
Shadows my tiny room with smouldering giants,
An arm is raised to fall which, falling, hurls
Hammer-blows forward rung with resonance;
And, shod with steel now, hear the hard hoof stamp.

GENEALOGY

1. *Ghost King*

My father is a ghost King:
                              he resides
In the shade of rain-drenched, green trees
That steal warmth from the sun's heat.
His realm is silence, ancient repose:
In darkness beneath the shadows which these stones
—Time-moulded and moss-softened—
Lean over, he holds sway.

The stream that runs on past his grave
Is Time, that lulls him in his sleep
Breeding abundance.
England by day is a green silence;
And beneath the grass, it is history runs on by: until
Night and my Father
Consume it.

Rags of the dawn-mist
Or shreds of bonfire-smoke
Shroud his dwelling, he is a ghost King,
His daylight apparition is the rainbow.

But mostly, his soul rests:
Under this hill crowned by the ancient church,
Where the dumb sheep attend him,
And sunlight flows like warm soft water over
Ancient sleep.

*

Come the night storm he is less liberal.
There is a spirit on the wind: is the voice his
That is howling beyond his grave,
Over the ravaged waste his *Lebensraum*—
Or the night air itself
In the bare branches of haggard trees and shrubs
That wails, sensing his coming?

Come the night storm his pastoral dream
Veers toward nightmare: after a lightning-flash,
Out of the darkness, like illumined smoke, there rises
An after-image of the scared beasts:
That are not sheep now, but horses, ghost horses—
Eyes ablaze, nostrils flared, ghastly unearthly white
Trampling a field of wetness
Stampeding the night's blackness.

A fleshless spirit is the stern conqueror;
Inclement in his triumph he tramples under
The dark, drenched, entangled shrubs
Whose roots are deep in mire.

And ghastly in whatever light should strike
The horses rear
Spurred by the English ghosts my Father's dream.

His dream is obsession. It is all-consuming.

2. *East Anglian Churchyard*

for Robert Wells

The land—low-lying, the fen drained—
still partakes of the flood, and the soil
of this green graveyard still has the swell,
the broken swell, of a calm sea, beneath which
graves are submerged.

And this church—dateless, its wall at a lean
and no tower—is a beached ship,
perhaps of northern pirates who having no more
rich coastal abbeys to fire, settling,
passed from the blue.

From the deep half-salvaged, there is one tombstone
rears above the surface where green leaf-light swims
in the shade of an oak-tree, ageless, ivied,
—and the stone entwined by the same ivy, its name
blotted by moss.

Beside recent deaths, no other stone
in sight—though here and there, a vague swell
covers a forgotten life. This
particular spot in the shade, he must have
chosen for memory.

3. *The Sons of the Invaders*

The path familiar, it will not lead back
—To un-build and to re-build—across carnage
To the strange beaches where our fathers' warships'
Prows cut crispness. For them the tide's backwash
Broke upon other shores, which now, for us,
Are drowned by the immensity they rode
At dispensation of the storm-god, eyes
Astrain—for land to yield infinities.

What have such dreams bequeathed us? Frost- and brine-tanged
Sagas of a long voyage; a universe
Of action like our fathers' in our scope;
And a rich soil that covers the repose
Of the deep-laid dead, who nourish other dreams
That burgeon here like childhood-memories
Of storm shattering sleep. Down at the thong
Of time's sequence, somewhere, a blade sung.

One of our bards' songs tells us of their landing:
The incandescent chalk cliffs' surge towards
A clear sky, now familiar, haunted by
Mist of the marshes they redeemed the land from
(This land, no more than that they lost us, ours)
To invest their virtue in it, so it yields us
Their richness, and their ghosts, malignant blooms:
Ghosts of our fathers, or our fathers' crimes?

4. *The Portrait*

Born in India where the sun glared
at the stoical English; his father's lip
stiff under the huge moustache, knit
with grizzled whiskers over the stiff
gilding of his red coat's collar; his mother,
haughty, decked in imperial silks,
her boned collar; the father's hands
so massive sinewed and scarred and no
soft lulling at the mother's breast:
a Victorian childhood, steel grey.

Sent back home to England: for hard
study and games under threat of the birch,
the runs before breakfast, the cold baths:
to make a man of him.
                                        And in his manhood
(before the Depression's grime, old age
and death) unfit for the Great War, tall
in Edwardian grey, a slight physique;
and his pale, melancholy, liberal eyes
fade from the picture looked at two wars past
by his son, who has no children, and remembers.

5. *Victorian Gothic*

for Dick Davis

Blackened walls: a Gothic height
Crouches and does not soar, locked
To the earth like slabs of outcrop stone
That touch no God; they imitate

Monoliths of the moors. Smokebound
Maze of streets in a northern town,
Low-skied misted marshland: ghosts
Haunt him, a grave imagination.

Mist merged with industrial smoke
Where the ghosts swim:
Their scrawny bodies topped with blackened heads
Like those that peer through jungle leaves.

Manufacturers, poets, moralists, colonisers, all
Engendered empires of despair
Built on blackness in the grey air.

What does the grey stone mask? Such battlements
Attest obscure defence.
                        His mind draws
Close to its melancholy: as
In dank winter to the heaped log-fire
Of a Saxon hall, beyond whose walls
What lurks in greyness?

Castles from dark days his reason
Girdles like siege but preserves,
Long years of siege that constitute defence;
Renascence ghosts, dark blood
Steams on the axe—industrial fumes
Dry the blood of the starved worker—marshland
Dank at sunset the sky bleeds
Pillarbox red.

THE NORTH LEGION

He wakes in the naked cold
In a place somewhere between night and morning.
Numb with hoar-frost, disarmed, his blood congealed
(Sealing the world behind encrusted eyes),
Blindly his body stirs.
Oblivion, still holding off the dawning,
Weighs warm on his stiff limbs and drugs his fears.

The horizon sharpens like a cruel surprise,
And like the sudden thought
That hardens in his memory with a shock
To an image firm as subterranean rock
Of the last battle he and his lost comrades fought:

A forest, dark, dappled with scattered shapes
Of pallid light, where the dust swirls and dances
Chaotic through the sunlight's slanting columns.
And here the legion marches
In order on the narrow natural path.
The occasional ray gleams
Sudden on armour, leaps
Through an ascending cloud of frosted breath,
Dissolves in darkness.

Till shadows of the northern gloom,
The shadows that resist each gleam,
Become material.
First animal
And furred it seems,
And then emergent violence
Of skin-swathed human forms.

They come with silence
And with icy pain.
They come to smash the barriers between
The dark repelled by armour and the dark entrenched within.

Along the hard horizon, the split sun's glare:
Overnight they have gone
Leaving a windswept moor, eroded bare.

The world he wakes to in his dereliction
Is mediated by no human dream
Of wonder or despair.

Rather it is a sheerness that is broken
—But sparsely, here and there—
By massed slabs of erupting outcrop stone:
Their edges dried and hard in the cold sun.

NORTHWARD

A hunter of the north, he follows
The mystery of the snows,
Weaving through blizzards'
Wavering streamers,
Tracing the paths of his uncertainty.

But, invading his body,
The wind's cold fingers
Steal through gaps in his furs
To conquer his warm detachment.
He lives on the moment

When the bullet strikes, the trap locks
Or the line tugs. He takes
Aim in the misty forest;
Breaks a hole in the ice,
Fishes in darkness.

THE RUINED ABBEY

And now the wind rushes through grassy aisles,
And over the massy columns the sky arches.

The monks who built it
Were acquainted with stone and silence.
Knowing the grandeur and endurance
Of isolated winter oaks, of rock,
And the hard rhythms of moors,
They retired here and reared it
From the crust of the north, moulding this form
Around their core of silence.

Their minds were landscaped.
Not with summer gardens that give sense ease
Nor beaches that lull questionings to a doze.
Their landscapes asserted agonies that
Probed them to the nerve;
The hardness of rock and the stream's ice
Formed a resistance they learned to resist,
To subdue, till it yielded
To silent movements of joy—
To the penetrating warmth of a mellow sun,
Its venerable eye.

The streams locked by ice,
The rocks, and the edged wind
Resisted their cowled will to define.
But resistance tautened questionings whose sinew
Shaped understandings.
The moor's silence snowed meanings,
And they knew that, while ice melts or cracks, they
Could endure like the rocks.

And so from the stone of landscaped minds, they fashioned
A form for those meanings, a form
That arched over meaningful air.

According to their time they shaped it
With massive grace.
And in the face of evil, weathers and decay
Its essence constant in the shiftings of ages.

And now the wind rushes through the grassy aisles,
And over the massy columns the sky arches.

In ruin, the form remains;
When the form falls, there is stone;
Stone crumbled, there is still
The dust, dust . . . and a silence
The centuries bow to, a silence
Lapped by the speechless howl of winds.

II

THE CLEARING

(1969-1975)

THE WELL

All day to gaze down into a well
as into yourself—as through self
to the blue sky fringed with green

of the world; and at length,
through a tunnelled forest of fronds that grow
from the mossy walls, to perceive

only your own face against the sky,
eyes glazed in contemplation, staring back
through a forest: is at large

to behold and desire to behold
—through foliage and from beyond darkness—
always, as in a well, meeting your stare,

your own face afloat on the surface,
with your thoughts bubbling from the deep spring
and your voice, reverberant, echoing response;

and to forget how without it
there is only the old perspective into endless dark
with silence at the source.

THE RECTOR

Naturalist, poet, priest
(1753-1830)

Privation for the poor
Was want of a shared soul,
And hungry intellect was stripped
Of serviceable role,

When in that partial Eden
The guardian of the Word
Had died, their pastor, who had named
The creatures of the Lord.

For the Word formed his thought,
His task to make collation
Of scripture with what quickened it,
The other book, creation;

And to the inward order
Thus answered, testify
In prose whose measured harmony
Compassed the butterfly;

Or verse that singled out
Familiar things: which could—
From prospect near or far—reveal,
In them, a primal good:

The truth he sought. Such fortune!
For love could move the search,
Till all that his attention held
Attended on his church

And drew toward the walls
Thick creepers still embrace,
Where chastened by the sombre yew
Light haunts his resting-place:

There once, a kind of pilgrim,
I thought how sad and mean
(Being shrunken to that yard and grove)
Was his once-fair demesne

And seeing the grave stones
As fragments of his store,
I felt—from hedgerow, evening air
And stream—his spirit soar

But met him in my own
Unsanctuaried spirit
Among the stones of an estate
I never shall inherit.

CHIVALRIC MONUMENT

I

Blithe, he appears where death
Has raised him: set on his tomb's pinnacle
To stir first memory then chronicle,
   He rides on air, arrayed in youth—
     Become, for his dead time,
     All manhood's paradigm;
His worn mortality is laid beneath.

II

From other shrines I cull,
In thought, to guard him, archangel and saint
Who stand—armed, gilded, and adorned with paint—
   As prayers their stone and bronze fulfill:
     Grave forms attenuated,
     Their dream-struck eyes averted,
Envisaging the beasts their bodies kill.

III

In youth he must have kneeled
To that august assembly of the spirit
And prayed to them for virtue, which would merit
   A throne like theirs. I as a child
     Mooned over books and pictures
     To strike chivalric postures
Alone, till time seemed for a time annulled.

IV

Did I dream—not in prayer—
Those honours, that unbroken heritage
Were for me? What between us seemed a bridge
  Now breaks, poised on the vacant air
    Where he rides free of time.
    Into a dream-space climb
Rider and horse, indifferent, debonair.

V

    I gaze up at his distance.
I arch my back, my body's almost steeled
To his bold pose—vainglorious as the child—
  But encounters its own resistance.
    He shakes his sword aloft
    And grins, as if he scoffed,
To glimpse this fretful, lorn, bemused existence.

'THE WEDDING OF ST GEORGE
AND PRINCESS SABRA'

His eyes that sought her eyes beyond her face,
His pale eyes with their nimbus of blond brows,
Have found what he had sought, through her embrace,
In the sky's pure infinity of blue.

Her eyes, which sought his heart through the wrought gold
Of burnished armour that defends their vows,
Find what he sees not under him—are held
By the set grin of the dark beast he slew.

ANDROMACHE

> '. . . as-tu pensé qu'Andromaque infidèle
> Pût trahir un époux qui croit revivre en elle . . .?
> Est-ce là cette ardeur tante promise à sa cendre?
> Mais son fils périssait: il l'a fallu défendre.
> Pyrrhus en m'épousant s'en déclare l'appui . . .'
>
> Racine, *Andromaque*, 1077-83

The future inconceivable—
Her hopes all dead except the last,
Her son; for his sake made a thrall
To Pyrrhus—with the noble past

(A voiceless ruin in the fires)
Claiming fidelity, she faced
Irreconcilable desires:
To foster life, to endure chaste.

ARTHUR DEAD

Terror stalks this land where once King Arthur
    Ruled with virtue steeped in vision;
Now in restless vigil his knights quest, their impulse
    Dark obsession.

Yet those few, who halting at the wayside
    Kneel to victims of the terror,
Salvage thus, from desolation which they ride in,
    Love and honour.

IN MALIGNANT TIMES

> 'Within this hollow vault here rests the frame
> Of that high soul which late informed the same,
> Torn from the service of the state in prime
> By a disease malignant as the time,
> Whose life and death designed no other end
> Than to serve God, his country and his friend,
> Who when ambition, tyranny and pride
> Conquered the age, conquered himself and died.'

> *Anon. Epitaph for James Rivers (died 1641) in the Priory
> Church of St Bartholomew the Great, Smithfield.*

1. *In Time of Civil War*

A Doctor: for the Time's disease
He knew no cure: though he could ease
This mind's unrest, that body's pain.
The makeshift home where he was sane
Housed tranquil dignity, that bore
Sober mistrust for Holy War.

The war he died in was not his:
Between two equal enemies
He chose to work withdrawn. But when
Ordered to sacrifice those men
—Patients and friends—who shared his home,
He chose to fight the war, alone.

Scorning promiscuous rhetoric,
With chaste formality he spoke:
The abstract words of his defence
Were tempered by experience,
No more: beyond that point he chose
The silence of secure repose.

2. *'Ein feste Burg'*

On a Lutheran pastor who preached against Hitler

The Time's demon had all but quelled
The faith he taught, to which he held
In doubt and hope. So he withdrew
To preach a version of the True:
Exiled within reality
To mediate lost sanctity.

When a Black Death of the spirit broke
Over Europe in blood and smoke
And silence, his Truth named as fact
What lucid empiricism lacked
Scope to envisage. A stronghold still
For him, his faith embraced the real.

His speech was action. The long quest
Of Europe's centuries seems compressed
Behind those words: which yet contain
In their calm voice his insight's pain;
Which drove hysteria and pride
Beyond the clearing where he died.

OF EPITAPHS

Not at peace with itself, in troubled times,
A divided mind might find sanctuary
Where yew-trees shade a field of scattered tombs
Subsidence tilts—or where an ambulatory,
Chill cavern of hewn stone, with grace recalls
Strife-proven virtue upon marble scrolls.

Might find, reposed in language that attests
To lives by death perfected, homages
Acclaiming perfect lives and certain rests.
Mere word and stone. Enduring images
Of what a culture trusted could be true
Or how such faith refracts what mortals do.

We though, our good a makeshift, may conceive
Of moral symmetry as mere simplesse
Or artifice—since we are bound to live
Poised between thought and what our thoughts address.
We, sceptics in our wisdom, miss their vice
Whose virtue, being substantial, could suffice.

DESERT WORDS

Some chose an alien clime
Whose sole association was despair

And qualified the land
With numb desolate words

Few men could understand
Or wish to hear

(Fragments of papyri, or desert sherds
No one could use)

To bide the passing of an alien time,
A time they did not choose.

LIKENESS

In John the Pisan's statue at Siena
Of the wolf suckling Romulus and Remus,
In the anxious eyes and searching nose—the low
Thrust of her gaunt head from the prominent spine,

I see my own dog: she, though sweetly pampered,
Looked drained and scrawny when, still half a puppy,
With bleeding teats, she bowed beneath her instinct
To mother her first brood: I see this much

As he, the sculptor, must have seen the she-wolf
And every burden dour fate lays on us
In the bent head of a spurned mongrel bitch
Upon the streets of Pisa or Siena.

MATERNITY

Until the tiny babe appears,
In the womb world a monster rears.
Pain is the magnitude she bears.

TWO INSCRIPTIONS

1. *The Goldsmith*

To stay anxiety I engrave this gold,
Shaping an amulet whose edges hold
A little space of order: where I find,
Suffused with light, a dwelling for the mind.

2. *Child of Nature*

for a roof-boss in a Gothic cathedral

Four oak-leaves from the dark behind his face
Sprout through his grin, and to this sacred place
Restore the primal counter-architecture,
Where four ribs hold and the head seals the structure.

TO THE UNDECEIVED

> '. . . to play the game of energetic barbarism . . .
> is, after all, a mental and moral impossibility.'
> Borges, *Other Inquisitions*

You who invoke survival, and condemn
To ruin all the crumbling palaces
And shady temples, where I seek the dim
Outline of order; who trust, that there is

Sufficient order in the wilderness
To harbour man, that unhistoric air
May yield desolate words, that consciousness
Must be most lucid sunk in black despair;

You are the more deceived of us: the night
Of your dark souls inherits a desire
That burns in you, as it were for the sight
To wearied Romans of their world on fire.
What answer you are the oncoming hordes
You'd join, at length to fall on your own swords.

Padua

SANCTUARY

Torcello Cathedral

On the massive grey stone shutters (by stone rings
Hinged to the Roman windows of the church walls)
Are scars that might be some wedged archaic script—
Through time obscured, through history part-deciphered.

Brooding on these, we conjure a day of trouble
When a mudflat, where grass grows amid brackish fens,
Grew from the mist, a blurred hope, barely risen
From the grey, tideless sleep of the lagoon.

For them though, a clear space, between fear and the sea:
For—the last walls of their larger fortress, Empire,
Fallen to Northern barbarians, to the Lombards—
They had fled to sea: to build their hopes on sand.

There from the crude substance of memories and images
And marble salvaged from the waste that was once their home,
They hewed a temple, draining the land around it:
Sowed crops there, bred beasts, drew fish from the sea.

And raised a high tower reaching above the mist,
Bell-tower and watch-tower, over the sea's languor:
And marine-dull chimes from the bell that called to prayer
Would call to safety women children and cattle

Into the fortress of their sanctity.
Then doors were barred and the slabs rolled over the windows
To bear their silent witness to Eastern arrows,
And the men went out to confront their older adversary:

Not purgers of decadence—the indifferent offspring
Of history, whose molten rush is cast in words—
But immemorial, grey ghost-marauders
That broke on the shore, grey spume of the ancient sea.

THE DISENCHANTED

On a painting by Atkinson Grimshaw,
'Liverpool Quay by Moonlight', 1887.

Riding at anchor ships from the New World,
Cargo-less now, sway, as in a trance;
Their lights float on a mist, their sails are furled;
They have disembarked both energy and distance.

Fated by deep unrest to haunt the quay
Aimless pilgrims, lit by the blear gaslight,
Emerge from haze, withdrawn in reverie:
        Exiles from day and night.

And at shop-windows they become transparent
To golden light that charms the brazen riches
There on display, before which they lament—
        As at vain reliquaries

That hold dead sanctity. They stare at distance
Imported by a manufactured world
To allure their wasting energy and substance
        By turning all to gold.

Bewitched but disenchanted lords they are,
Of a legendary treasure long since dispossessed,
Who drift with the dissolving atmosphere—
        Dim shades of the lost.

Only the lamp on a black, advancing coach
—Unearthly green!—can focus in reflection,
Composing all you see as you approach:
Light of the mind it stays from desolation.

THE GRAIL KNIGHT

I

To his Lady

I leave you to return. No other love
Draws me from our still clearing, from your side.
Though unassured, I go but to abide
Some answer to my question; and I move

Into the forest that I woke to see
Turned to a labyrinth of broken night
By paths of afterglow, a weird pale light
Whose dissolution is my memory.

It is in quest of the light's source, my love,
That I must leave here, armed in my cold mail:
Only the knight who seeks the Holy Grail
Can sanctify the space where he would live.

II

Beyond the clearing where my true love stays
Passions allure me from my proper path:
I hack my way through thorn, I waste my breath
In a dark, tortuous, subterranean maze,

And lose myself, and fall into despair.
Then, by chance, my inconstant eyes behold
A gorgeous relic—moss-bound—worked in gold.
Its patient fretwork concentrates my stare,

As if its web of glimmerings enshrined
The broader light it answers—that which glows
Beyond this changing palisade of trees,
And whose slow radiance occupies my mind.

III

Far in the wood in the eye of a quiet pool—
Where I dismount, to satisfy my thirst—
Images of the flame I follow, burst
Into white flares. I cannot see the Grail.

In thirst leaning toward that element
I see, dissolved in it, my own pale face
Illumined there beyond my reach—such grace
Enraptures it that, here, I must lament.

In wonder now I bend to question me,
And I am answered when toward me rise
My love's redeeming underwater eyes;
From whose lips, dreamed, I drink reality.

OCTOGENARIAN

The dead survive in words,
The dark beneath their light.
   Memory's shards
Are bright stars that compose the night.

The magic words she mutters
Summon from her deep past
   People and matters
Whose substance memories outlast.

Beyond fact, contemplating
Pageants that crowd her thought—
   Her words creating
Pale shades of loves whose warmth they sought—

She lives entranced, but with
A cold weight on her mind
   That is not death,
That is the dead she cannot find.

THE LAKE

The grey lake, toward the centre, darkens.
An innocent, whose spirit harkens
To rumour of despair, stops here;
She weeps, seduced by nameless fear.

All half-forgotten time, all dreams
—Like audible but unseen streams—
Fall to this depth of black depression.
She is the victim of obsession,

And knows it—helplessly aware
That ancient mire, layer formed on layer,
Absorbs her soul: she cannot break
Free of the tangles beneath the lake,

Free of the tangles in her mind
That bind her and, through her, her kind
And the whole planet, at the last,
To a cruel, inauthentic past.

THE RICHES

The boy stares down between planks where the swell
  Smacks sheer against the bulwarks, then subsides:
Leaving beneath his pier a kind of well
Of pulsing water, the broad ocean quelled
  To a swirling stillness lost amid the tides.

A light, drawn ghostly down to the sea-bed,
  Refracted, finds unfading colours there,
That draw the boy's mind down, flooding his head,
Staining the water as they shift and spread.
  Immersed in wonder, he draws back, in fear,

From plunging toward the object of his praise
  (To probe the alien silence and explore
  An under-world with no perspective law
Where blurred eyes wildly stare in a salt haze)

And gazes at the riches, void of speech
  And every sense but sight; and longs to soar
  Back through the waves to bright air, swim ashore,
And lay the spoils in sunlight on the beach.

BIRD - WATCHER

It returns to the same nest. The watcher lies
Beneath spring brushwood to await its coming—
At watch so long he dreams himself becoming
Less than himself and more, the landscape's eyes.

Though far beyond his eyes, beyond the range
Of field-glasses, he knows it breaks no bonds:
Its instinct to his knowledge corresponds,
Riding the current of the season's change.

What is there in a small bird's blood that learns
To plot its course by sun and stars, being drawn
Yearly toward a lost, remembered dawn?
The watcher broods on this. The bird returns.

And all its colours flash where he attends—
A deep blue, mantling rust and white—, it sings
Caged in his retina; then, on curving wings,
Veers off to vanish where the human ends.

THE MARINER'S WIFE

I

She is his sleeping partner: the dawn tide,
That drowns her, is the sea his vessels ride.

Dissolved into his thoughtless recollection,
She calms his image in the sea's reflection;

And yet his sailors, anxious when storms lour,
Fear the awakening of her dormant power.

II

The capricious will, it is, of the sea god
Provokes the vagrant impulse of her blood.

Tangles and sounding silence, broken light
And shifting currents, overruled by night:

These are her world—an undetermined space,
Littered with sunken gems, fallen from grace.

III

His eyes reflect wide blues of sea and sky.
She, cat-like in her darkness, is light-shy.

But when toward sunset he retrieves his vision
Her eyes meet his, and then—before illusion

(Night casting her up) can wander free—
Their wedded vision is reality.

ROMANCE

for Diane

My dreams once met you tangled in the snare
Set by the world-dragon; and then redeemed
By me, you were, to walk in the free air
Of the immaculate chivalry I dreamed—
Yet subject to nightmare.
   One night we'd walk through gardens of my vision;
   The next, through deserts of my will's confusion.

Now you have met me dreams must die, for there,
In half-clear-sighted impotent illusion,
Your life and meaning stumble, and the air
Breathed by your innocence is through delusion
Polluted by despair.
   My love, I know: you are not what you seemed
   And have not walked the wastes I dreamed.

THE CLEARING

Between the dark and us there stands
A silent guard, whose sword commands
   The forest powers, to keep
Back from the clearing where we sleep.

Since an historic dawn, unseen
He's kept watch camouflaged in green.
   The night we need not fear.
By day I hunt and leave you here.

Your body to a hunter's mind
Is anchorage, for here you tend
   All we have understood
And held against the anarchic wood—

A clearing, where love grows, and rests.
In ignorance one fear molests
   Our separateness: that he,
Our guard, might turn our enemy.

Wild from his timeless vigil, rage
Might free him from the thorny cage:
   So long held in reserve
His energies, which now preserve,

Would waste the clearing and, impelled
By forces he from night dispelled,
   He'd thus, from earth razed bare,
Regenerate extinct despair.

SAXON BUCKLE

in the Sutton Hoo treasure

His inlaid gold hoards light:
A gleaming thicket to expel,
With intricacy worked by skill,
The encroaching forest night
Where monsters and his fear dwell.

Gold forest tangles twined by will
Become a knot that closes in
The wild beasts that begin
Beyond his habitation.
An object for his contemplation.

—From which three rivets gaze:
A beast's head forested within,
That clasps his swordbelt to his breast
By daylight, and before his eyes,
By hearthlight, stills unrest.